THE HOPPINGOOD™ RABBIT FAMILY in

Hoppin' Healthy Harvesters

BY CYNTHIA HAIGH

ILLUSTRATED BY CARRIE ANNE BRADSHAW

A Li'l Woodzeez™ Book

To Jennifer and Caroline

Edited by Joanne Burke Casey.

ISBN: 978-0-9843722-8-7
Printed in China.

Welcome to Honeysuckle Hollow

where all the woodland creatures work together
to take care of each other and their environment.

Every animal family has a special job and every day is an adventure. With their creativity, generosity and sweet spirit, these friends make chores chockfull of fun.

Meet all the Li'l Woodzeez™ families
in the back of this book.

Star and Theo Hoppingood, and their parents, Amelia and Elliot, scampered to their blueberry patch to pick the plump, ripe blueberries.

They had a big problem.

The Bushytail family needed lots of berries to make oodles of their famous blueberry pies for the Honeysuckle Hollow Sunflower Celebration the next day.

But the Hoppingoods were worried.

Would they be able to pick enough berries for the Bushytails on time?

All of a sudden they heard twigs snapping and footsteps coming from the brush. Star and Theo were afraid.

Amelia and Elliot tried to calm them. They knew it had to be one of their friends stopping by to help.

Sure enough, it was Suds Tidyshine, whistling merrily and making his way through the bushes.

Word had spread throughout Honeysuckle Hollow that the Hoppingoods needed extra helping hands.

Suds was eager to join in. Elliot gave him a basket and Suds quickly got started.

Star and Theo continued to pick the berries. But after awhile they began to get really hungry.

Their tummies rumbled and grumbled.

"Let's eat just a handful of berries," whispered Star.

"Let's eat just a handful of berries," whispered Star, as she and her brother sat on a stump behind the bushes.

They began to eat the delicious, juicy fruit from the basket they shared.

They talked and laughed and ate. After a few minutes they realized they had eaten every berry in the basket.

"Oh no! What do we do now?" asked Star.

"I guess we're going to have to tell Mom and Dad," she said, answering her own question.

Suds was picking berries at a nearby bush and happened to overhear Star.

HOPPIN' HEALTHY HARVESTERS
FARM STAND

"I wouldn't worry too much," he said. "I have a cart *loaded* with berries. It's enough to feed everybody in Honeysuckle Hollow!"

He led the Hoppingoods to the other side of the bushes.

There stood his cart, overflowing with blueberries brought from his home.

"Mr. Tidyshine, why did you bring so many berries from your garden?" asked Amelia.

"I knew you were worried about getting the berries picked in time for the Bushytails to make their delicious pies," Suds replied. "And my yard was overgrown with berries."

"I love their pies as much as anyone else," Suds laughed.

"I wanted to give them to the Bushytails. I love their pies as much as anyone else," Suds laughed. "In fact, I hope to scoop up a piece of every one of their pies at the Sunflower Celebration!"

That night, Suds and the Hoppingoods delivered the cart and baskets of fresh berries to the Bushytails.

The Bushytails were so grateful for all the fruit.

Maggie Bushytail reached
into her cupboard and filled
five baskets with biscuits
and berry jam.

The Hoppingoods and Suds
were thrilled to have had
two harvests that day.

"What a berry nice day," said Theo.

“We gathered berries from *our berry patches* and the Bushytails gathered treats from *their cupboards*!” said Star.

“What a berry nice day,” said Theo. They all laughed. It was a berry nice day indeed.

Collect all the Li'l Woo

The Waterwaggle™ Beaver Family

Busy Beaver Launderette

Tapper and Tiny gather the freshly washed laundry off the clothesline and can't help burying their faces in the crisp bed sheets. Their parents, Lulu and Bobby, put up with their antics, but don't realize how important "sniffing the sheets" will become in Honeysuckle Hollow.

The Handydandy™ Mouse Family

Bitty Fix-It Crew to the Rescue

When something breaks in Honeysuckle Hollow, the woodland creatures skedaddle to the Bitty Fix-It Shop. That's where Mimi and Benjamin, and their kids, Nibbles and Sunny, repair just about anything. From squeaky school desks to broken kites, they're the go-to fix-it mice.

The Bushytail™ Squirrel Family

Tickle-Your-Taste-Buds Bakers

The Tickle-Your-Taste-Buds Bakery makes the most scrumptious pies in town. Maggie and Oliver, along with their kids, Henry and Honeybun, pick and peel apples while Grandma Agnes gets the pie crusts ready. Then it's time to deliver their pies on a bicycle built for two.

›ZEEZ™ FRIENDS & BOOKS

The Whooswhoo™ Owl Family

Nighty-Night-Sleep-Tight Safety Service

Delores and Owen, and their kids, Pete and Peep, can see all over town from their watchtower. It's important that everything's in order in Honeysuckle Hollow. One day, after cousin Keith slips on banana peels, they investigate and find a trail of peels that leads to a mystery.

The Whiffpuff™ Skunk Family

Fresh-as-a-Daisy Air Quality Patrol

Thanks to Jasmine and Jacob, and their twin daughters, Iris and Violet, Honeysuckle Hollow smells wonderful. The skunk family picks flowers, berries, herbs and spices, then creates special scents and soaps. Iris and Violet like bathtime, too. Rub-a-dub-dub, two skunks in a tub!

The Tidyshine™ Turtle Family

Clean-as-a-Whistle Tidying Service

Dishes don't stay dirty long in Honeysuckle Hollow. Suds and Sally, and their children, Buster and Bubbles, zip from one kitchen to the next on roller skates. They've earned a spotless reputation for scrubbing pots and pans until every last one is clean.

The Swiftysweeper™ Hedgehog Family

Sweep, Mop, Sparkle & Shine Specialists

When May and Whoosh are too busy cleaning floors, they get their twins, Moppy and Dusty, to help. They're hard workers but cannot resist the opportunity to have some fun. After a mishap that results in a visit to the health center, they realize that life is not all work and no play.

The Hoppingood™ Rabbit Family

Hoppin' Healthy Harvesters

Amelia and Elliot are picking blueberries at their farm. When their children, Star and Theo, get hungry, they decide to eat a few of the ripe berries. But one handful leads to another and soon the whole basket is empty! Will there be enough for everyone in Honeysuckle Hollow now?

The Diggadilly™ Raccoon Family

Reduce, Reuse & Recycle Crew

Debbie and Stripe Diggadilly, and their parents, Rose and Rocco, hate to see anything go to waste. Their business, the Reduce, Reuse & Recycle Crew, specializes in making treasures out of trash and art gems out of junk. All it takes is a little imagination and elbow grease. When Debbie and Stripe find an old fence at the dump, they also find a clever solution to a problem for their classmates.